© TORVA
Heroes of the Vegetable Patch
Project manager: Lena Allblom, IKEA FAMILY
Project co-ordinator: Anders Truedsson, TITEL Books AB
Text: Ulf Stark
Illustrations: Charlotte Ramel
Graphic design: Pierre Österholm
Typesetting: Gyllene Snittet
International editor: Janet Colletti, Boco Text Studio/Boco AB
Translation: Comactiva Translations AB, Sweden
Produced by IKEA FAMILY
Paper: Symbol Freelife Satin FSC
Printing: Litopat S.p.A, Italy 2011

Ulf Stark   Charlotte Ramel

Heroes of the Vegetable Patch

"The children are coming!" murmurs the broccoli.

"Oh no, it's going to get scary!" murmurs the carrot.

The vegetables lean to one side as best they can. They're afraid of the children's feet.

The wild strawberry hides behind a stone and pulls its hat down over its eyes.

"It's nice to see you out playing," says the old lady. "But you have to watch where you're walking."

She lives in the house next door to the children. It's her vegetable patch.

"Okay," says Erik.

"We'll be careful," says Eva.

Because those are the children's names.

The next day their ball goes over the hedge. It lands right next to a row of terrified dill plants.

"Will they ever learn?" grumbles the carrot.

"I hope the old lady gives them a good scolding," says the broccoli.

"Sorry, it was an accident," says Erik.

"I know. You're only having fun, and it's easy to forget to be careful," says the old lady, and then she gives a sigh.

"What's the matter?" wonders Eva.

"My sister is not feeling well. I have to go away so I can take care of her."

When the old lady has gone away, the children play in the vegetable patch every day. There are so many great places to hide.

Eva hides behind a redcurrant berry bush.

"Gosh it's hot, isn't it?" the redcurrants murmur.

"Yes it is, and we're not getting any water," sighs the broccoli. "I'll be turning all yellow and horrible soon. Nobody will want me."

"And I'll soon fall off my plant," says the strawberry.

But Eva doesn't realize that. Because when plants talk, it just sounds like a murmur.

But she can see that the plants' leaves are drooping.

And she thinks their murmurs sound a little bit sadder than before.

"We ought to help the old lady," says Eva to Erik when he finds her. "Otherwise the plants will die, and what will she live on then?"

"That's a good idea. But we don't know anything about fruit and vegetables," he says. "Imagine if we could shrink down and ask them ourselves."

"No sooner said than done," says the carrot, because he can do magic.

He simply says BIG backwards and the children become small.

First they shrink down to the size of cucumbers. Then potatoes.

And finally to the size of radishes.

"Gosh you're ever so small," laughs Eva.

"You too!" says Erik.

Then he gives a tremendous shriek! Because up from the ground comes an enormous head! And then a gigantic wriggly body!

"Help!" he cries. "An enormous snake!"

He grabs Eva by the hand so they can run away.

But the plants just laugh. Especially the tomato, who hits his big round red tummy.

"That's just the earthworm," he says. "He's our very best friend. He makes the soil all nice for our roots."

"I knew that," says Erik, laughing as much as he can.

The parsley and dill plants wave like tree tops above Erik and Eva's heads.

"What do you want?" wonders the carrot.

"We want to help," says Erik. "You're all starting to look dry and withered."

"Just tell us what to do," says Eva.

"Well first of all we need water," says the broccoli. "Otherwise we can't even talk."

The next day Eva and Erik have rubber boots on.
They each brought a shovel and a rake with them.
"Okay," they say. "Let's get started."
"Excellent," says the carrot.
And he says "GIB" which is… something backwards. Do you know what?

Every afternoon the children come to the vegetable patch and get to work.
"I hope the old lady comes back soon," says Eva.
"Me too," says Erik. "My whole body is tired."
"So's mine," says Eva. "It's still fun though."
They fetch water from a tub and pour it on the soil.
They clear weeds and put them on the compost heap.
They rake the walkways so they're nice and neat.
And above their heads the bumblebees buzz away, like little round airplanes.

When they've finished their work for the day, they play with the young fruit and vegetables.
They play football with a berry.
They swing on a spider's silk.
And then they climb up onto the rhubarb, and lie down to rest on the big leaves.
"Saturday is market day," says the strawberry. "I wonder if the old lady will be back by then."

But she isn't.

Everyone helps fill a wheelbarrow with ripe fruit and vegetables.
But just then, they hear someone calling.
"Help me! Help me!" cries a dark voice.
It's the bumblebee, who has fallen into the water and can't get out.
It is lying on its back fluttering its wings frantically.
"I can't make it much longer!" it says.

So Erik and Eva jump in. Good thing they can swim! They have a large
rhubarb leaf with them as they swim up to the bumblebee.
"Crawl up onto this," they say.
And they help push so the bumblebee can get on properly.

Once the bumblebee has dried off, it can fly again.
"You saved my life," it says.
"Yes, you're the heroes of the vegetable patch," says the carrot.
"I'd never have believed it."
"Neither would we," says Eva. "But we'd better hurry, or we won't
make it to the market."

"Come and get your fruit and vegetables!" shouts Erik.
And Eva is in charge of the money, because she's the best at counting.
They sell potatoes and dill and parsley. And carrots, broccoli, and berries.
Everyone wants to buy the children's fruit and vegetables.
They keep the money in a cashbox.

The evening before the old lady is due back, the fruit and vegetables
hold a party for the children. The glowworms glow between the leaves.
The cricket plays his music, and the earthworm dances a dance.
"Thank you for taking such good care of us," says the carrot.
"Yes, we really are very grateful," says the broccoli.
"Hooray for the heroes of the vegetable patch!" says the strawberry.
And it blushes under its white hat with red spots.
Later, the children get to take a ride on the bumblebee's back.

When the old lady comes home, she's both happy and sad at the same time.
Happy because her sister is feeling better again.
But sad when she thinks about her vegetable patch.
"All my fruit and vegetables have probably withered," she says when Erik and
Eva greet her at the gate. "It's been so hot."
"Yes, it certainly has been hot," says Erik.
"And no rain," says the old lady.
"No, not a drop," says Eva.

When the old lady sees the vegetable patch, she doesn't say anything at first.
Then she gets tears in her eyes. Tears of joy! She breathes in deeply to smell all
the lovely smells.
"Was it you who saved my fruit and vegetables?" she asks.
"Well, we helped out a bit," says Eva.
"I don't know what to say," says the old lady, drying her eyes.
"Just say thank you," says Erik.

And he hands her the cashbox full of money.
"Well goodness gracious me! I don't know *what* to call you!"
"Call us the heroes of the vegetable patch," says Eva.
And all around them, the plants give a warm murmur.
"Thank you ever so much. Come back tomorrow!" they say.